THE PROBLEM IS....

ISBN: 979-8-9863710-5-4 (Paperback)

ISBN: 979-8-9863710-7-8 (Hardcover)

Permission to use material:

Photos/Vectors - www.vecteezy.com

Illustrator: MD Bellal Hussain

Editor: Tram Bui

Credits for the cover design: Amy_Creative (www.fiverr.com)

Printed in the United States of America.

For more information or requests, please email the author at worldprofessor1@gmail.com .

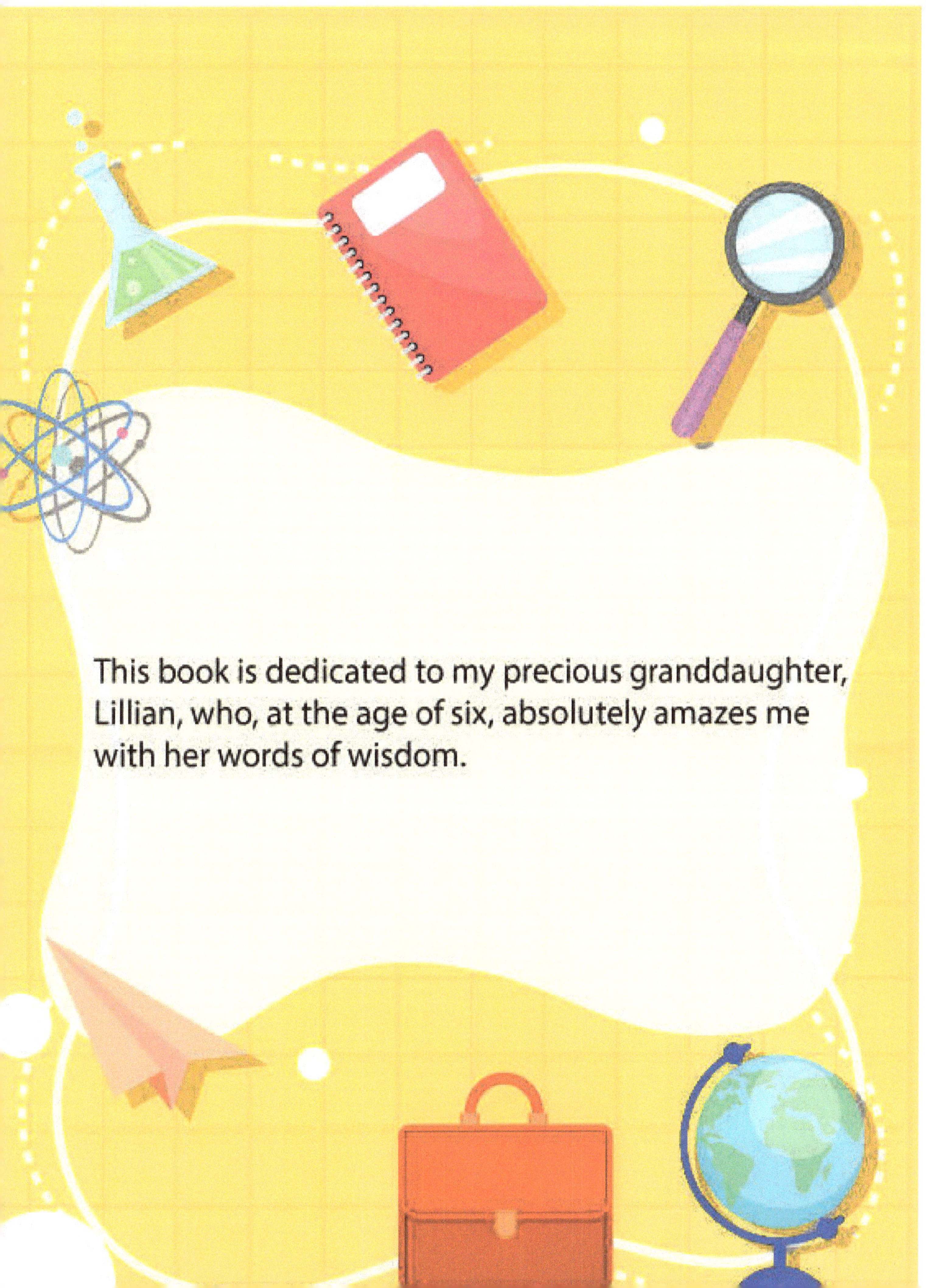

This book is dedicated to my precious granddaughter, Lillian, who, at the age of six, absolutely amazes me with her words of wisdom.

My name is Molly. I am six-years-old and in kindergarten.
I want to be a detective when I grow up.

I like doing cartwheels, playing on the trampoline, playing with Legos, building towers with blocks, and playing games on the tablet.

My brother's name is Nate. He likes to read about axolotls. He also likes to play games on the tablet.

Axolotls

An axolotl is like a salamander that lives in the water and has six gills, three on each side of its body, to breathe.

The axolotl looks like it is smiling all the time.

Nate wants to be a scientist when he grows up.

Sometimes, I get into trouble. I don't like being in trouble. I think it is because I have lots of energy, like ants.

When I get mad, I go to my room and lock the door. I sit on the carpet and fold my arms.

As I am upset, Mom, Dad,

Pe-Pa (that is what I call my grandfather)

or

Me-Me (this is what I call my

grandmother) asks me to unlock

the door.

Pe-Pa and Me-Me ask me, "What is the matter?"

I tell them, "The problem is...

My first problem is:

"I AM FLUSTERATED" because I cannot win my game!"

My second problem is:

"It is not fair! They are not playing with me. So, I go to my room, sit on the carpet, and pout."

My third problem is:

"They are rudies!"

My fourth problem is:

"No one listens."

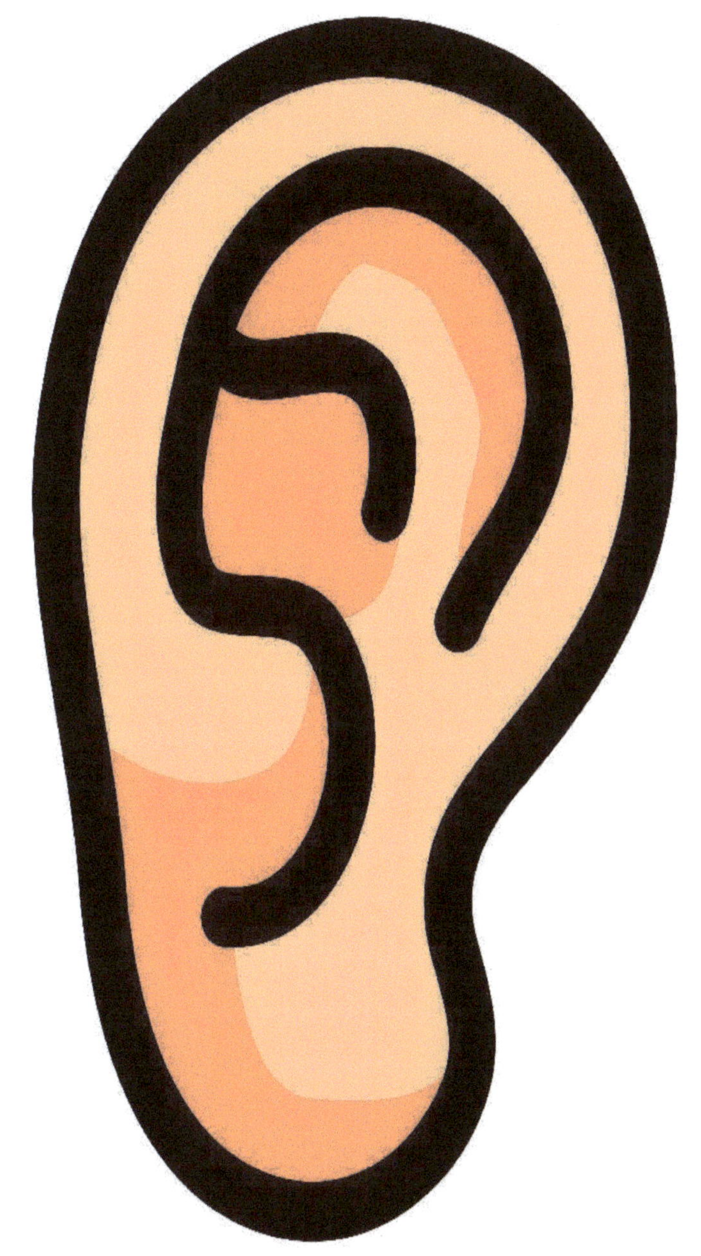

My fifth problem is:

"My tablet needs to be charged. It is at 90."

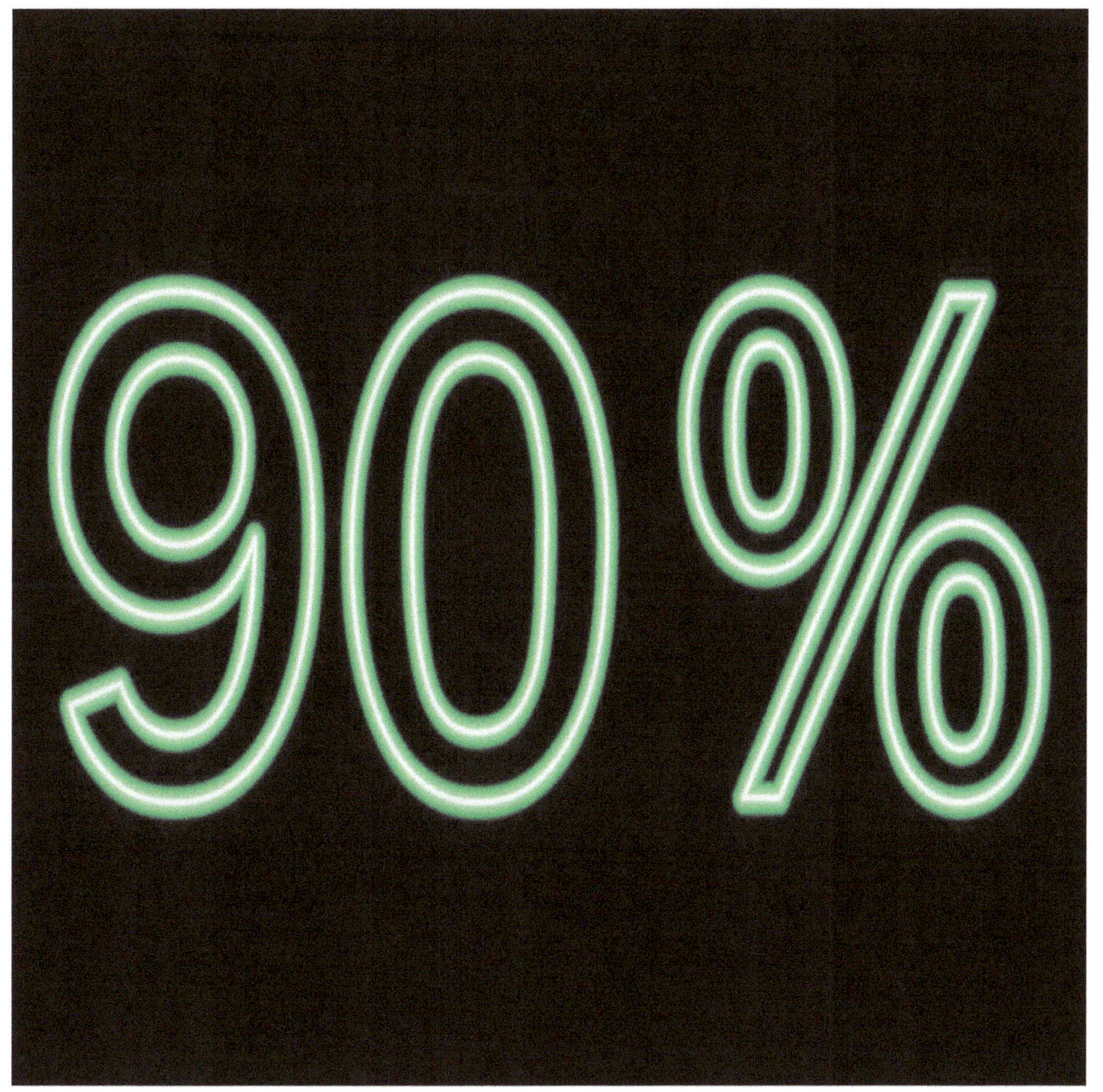

My final problem is:

"When I go over to

Pe-Pa and Me-Me's house at 47,

there are no bananas, cheese sticks, or

jello. These are my favorite snacks!"

How can I fix these problems?

Me-Me and Pe-Pa know I want to be a detective.

They ask me to be a detective by finding
plastic eggs.

"I just know there is something in there."

FIRST EGG

I found the first egg in the kitchen.

There was a chocolate in it.

There was a note, too. Me-Me read it to me.

It said, "Take a deep breath in through your nose and out through your mouth." So, I did.

TAKE A DEEP
Breath

I have asked Me-Me and Pe-Pa to do this, too, so I know all about this.

I was off to hunt for the next egg.

I said, "Detective Molly is on the case!"

SECOND EGG

I found the second egg near a chair in the living room.

I loved the jellybeans in this egg. There was a note in the plastic egg. The note in the egg said, "Count to ten." So, I did.

I am off to hunt for the next egg.

I said, "Detective Molly is on the case!"

Third Egg

I found the next egg outside the door.

There was a gummy bear and a note in the egg.

This note said, "Stop what you are doing, and come back to it later."

STOP

I did not know what this meant, so I asked Me-Me about it. She said I had to stop, put the egg down, and come back to get it later.

COME
BACK

Me-Me said the lesson here is "Stop when you get frustrated and come back to what you were doing later."

Welcome
BACK

So, this means I need to take a break.

Take
a
BREAK

I was off to search for the next egg.

I said, "Detective Molly is on the case!"

Egg

The fourth egg was hard to find, but I found it upstairs on a shelf in my bedroom.

There was a gum drop in the egg with a note. It said, "Hold and squeeze a stuffed animal that you like." So, I squeezed my bear.

I was off to find the next egg.

I said, "Detective Molly is on the case!"

Fifth Egg

I found the fifth egg near my mom's desk.

This egg had a piece of hard candy and a note in it.

The note said, "Listen to music."

"I love to sing and listen to music. So, I started to sing a song about primary and secondary colors.

This hunt is so exciting. I am off to find the next egg. Me-Me and Pe-Pa said, "Detective Molly is on the case!"

Last Egg

I found the last egg. It was outside.

There was a piece of candy corn and a note in it.

The note said, "Go and play!"

PLAY...

I found six eggs in all!

"I am Detective Molly, and I'm on the case!"

Can you think of some other clues to
help me solve problems? Thank you!

With your help, we have solved the case.

"We make a great team."

AAH! I FEEL BETTER NOW!

FEEL
GOOD

Afterword:

Mark H. McCraw has spent more than a decade in education, working with children and students of all ages, from infants to college students. He is an Air Force/Air Force Reserves Disabled Veteran. Mark is a father of four adult children and a grandfather of nine grandchildren. He lives in Oklahoma.

Currently, Mark is a member of the Society of Children's Book Writers and Illustrators (SCWBI), Alliance of Independent Authors (AIA), Oklahoma Literacy Association (OLA), Oklahoma Library Association (OLA), American Library Association (ALA), Korea Defense Veterans Association (KDVA), American Legion, Veterans of Foreign Wars (VFW), and the Disabled American Veterans (DAV) Jr. Vice Commander.